Poems for Children

(and silly people...)

Barry Robinson

A note on the illustrations

The illustrations for these poems have been secured by purchasing a license to use the images from depositphotos.com and other such sites. The drawings to some of the 'Book of Nonsense' writings, nursery rhymes not to mention a few of the miscellaneous poems, like 'Beards' for example, are by the great Edward Lear.

Copyright © 2019 by Barry Robinson

All rights reserved. No part of this publication may be reproduced, distributed, or transmitted in any form or by any means, including photocopying, recording, or other electronic or mechanical methods, without the prior written permission of the publisher, except in the case of brief quotations embodied in critical reviews and certain other non-commercial uses permitted by copyright law.

Any likeness to anyone living or dead in these poems is purely coincidental.

ISBN: 9781673193855

Contents

My Favourite Words	1
Hedgy Hog	2
Bear Hunt	3
The Boozle Fish	5
The History of Custard	6
The Gumble Snoop	8
Your First Words	10
My Imagination	11
Frog	13
Bubbles	14
Little Lily Pinky	16
Beards	17
Cucumbers	19
Little Tommy Tumpkins	20
He Gave Names to the Animals	22
Snuggly Shmuggly Boo	24
Spiders are funny	25
My Neighbour's dog	27
The Knights of Foozalah	28
The Planets	33
My Teacher's a Cannibal	35

Book of Nonsense

Old Miss Hipkiss	39
The Owl & the Pussy Cat	41
More Nonsense	43

Nursery Rhymes
(The Dead Sea Scrolls)

Dr Foster	49
Hey Diddle Diddle	50
Hickery Dickery Dock	51
Humpty Dumpty	52
Incy Wincy Spider	53
Jack & Jill	54
Jack be Nimble	55
Little Bo Peep	56
Little Miss Muffet	57
Mary, Mary	58
Sing a Song a Sixpence	59
The Grand Old Duke of York	60
This Little Piggy	61

A Sweet Tooth	63
Pies are Great!	65
Five Sisters	67
Christmas Acrostic	69
Bottoms are Funny	70
Goldilocks Got an ASBO	71
I Wish I Were a Tree	73
Making Lists	74
The Marillos	76
Our Little Snorer	77
The Greedy Puss	79
Princess Frog Snogger	80
Rhapsody in Pink	81
Sausages	82
Simile Song	83

Teddington	84
Smile Train	85
Terrence Rex	86
Snowflakes	87
Summer Days	88
Fingers McFilcher	89
Nicola Pickle-a	91
Widgity-Fidgity	92
The Mouse Thief	93
The Sea	95
A Train Journey	97
Vegetables	99
Words	100
I Love Pickles	102
My Toilet is Haunted	103
Elephants	105
Cloud Gazing	106
The End	108

Introduction

Coleridge said that poetry is comprised of the best words in the best order. I cannot claim that these are the 'best' words, or even the 'best' order for that matter. They are mere observations of the increasingly silly and absurd world I inhabit; all collected together to amuse my own little brood.

For it is good to be children sometimes...

Charles Dickens

My Favourite Words

Kerfuffle! Is a fabulous word.
With plenty of *fuffle* to it.
It starts with the *ker* -
Before the fluffy bit
Rounds it all up,
Lickety-split.

And squiggle has a *squig*
And an *iggle*,
That giggles and tickles
And squigs and wriggles.

Bubble is like bibble
With plenty of *ubble*.
Plosives and explosives
That pop and impound -
Droplets and poplets,
Resound and drown
In rounds of sound.

Hedgy Hog

Up pops the moon and sometime soon
A prickly personage arrives for tea.
He
   Sniffles-
   Snuffles -
   And stamps his feet,
 Hoping for a meaty treat.

He looks for worms and things that squirm.
He
   Slurps –
   Burps -
   Chomps and heaves,
And drops little sausages on top of the leaves.

Across the lawn he hoofs and hoofs - prickles All spruced -
      And barges and barges
      Through forests of rhubarb.

    He:

    Fluffles –
    Wiffles-
    Waddles –
    Sniffles -
    And rolls himself into a ball.
    He watches with one eye prised open…
    And pretends not to be there at all.

Bear Hunt

My daughter loves the 'Bear Hunt'
Almost every single night –
With its:
Squishy -
Squashy -
Squelchy-ness.
A quirkiness that's *'Outta sight!'*

She performs all the actions with gusto
As if straight from the Royal Ballet -
She runs up the stairs,
To hide from the bear,
Beneath her mother's duvet.

Rivers to pass and long wavy grass,
As she jumps from leaf to leaf.
With blizzards and hazards,
Her wits are gathered,
As she fumbles with the usual motif –

That is:

A girl, a wood, and great big bear.
But no porridge, bed or broken chair.
No Baloo, honey and bright red balloons,
Like numerous bears in numerous cartoons.

This time it is she and she alone -
Amid the mystery of this intriguing tome.

> She tiptoes into the forest,
> In search of the beastly abode,
> Stumble trip!
> Stumble trip!
> Into the forest she goes.

Then:

Amidst the swirling whirling snowstorm -
On not 'such a beautiful day' -
She drifts away to Dozy Land –
And quietly floats away -
To the patter of paws and
Pillows of snores,
Where the trees will softly say…

*"It's time for bed sleepy head.
No more bear hunt for you today."*

But:

She tosses and turns and studiously learns
Every phrase and stride without fail,
As she embarks upon that enchanting trek
That is Mr. Rosen's grizzly tale.

The Boozle Fish

The Boozle fish burbles
   And bubbles
   And nibbles your toes.

   He splashes and splishes
    The smaller fishes -
   He bounds and he sploshes
    And shamelessly noshes
      At all living things in his way.

  The Boozle fish is a little bit snippy
And sniffs out a tasty bite.
He likes to nibble at nippers
  That paddle in rivers
     And gobbles them up in the night.

The History of Custard

The year was 1410,
When some thick set men,
All found the biscuits a tad dry.
What they need is a sauce -
That the king could endorse -
To soak his wife's apple pie.

The Duke of Cardiminia,
Begged his wife from Sardinia,
For something to smother his pud.
He was tempted by cream and would often dream
Of something that was wholesome and good.

His Duchess began stirring -
And the kitties were purring -
As a quart of milk was stirred in.
The cows formed a queue with a series of *Moooos!*
And their bells made a calamitous din.

The concoction was gloopy,
And a little bit soupy,
When the royal tasting would begin.
Alas! - It was pale and lacked texture -
And was unlikely to pleasure -
So stately chickens were drafted in.

They knew what to do
To add the right hue.
And laid with all they could muster.

With a squeeze and a cluck
The Duke was in luck,
And presented with a prototype 'Custer.'

Yes, the sauce was named 'custard' -
As it rhymed with mustard -
And made the rendering of this poem a breeze.
It was named after Buster
The Duke's favourite jester
And thickened by his wife's best trapeze -

Who leapt and bounded
Until the product was pounded
Into shape for king's hard-working cooks.
This brand new invention,
Had a custardy intention
Of making the court's history books.

It was presented to the king -
And the angels did sing -
Of puddings, tarts and buns.
The Duke of Cardiminia –
And his wife from Sardinia
Were honoured along with their sons.

Oceans of custard and time has passed
Since the first royal pud majestically basked
In that glorious, glutinous splodge!
From spotted dicks, traditional plum duff,
Children are badgered and ferociously stuffed
With heaps of yellow, syrupy stodge.

The Gumble Snoop

The Gumble Snoop is a funny beastie
Who harbours a devious plan.
He dances at night -
And is a dreadful fright -
Feasting on dry bread and spam.

The Gumble Snoop is a nasty chap
Who endeavours to make lots of money.
He needles the bees,
And tickles their knees,
Before running away with their honey.

The Gumble Snoop is an odd looking fellow
Who babbles such a frightful blether.
With long bony toes,
And knees that bow,
That are constantly knocking together.

The Gumble Snoop is a crafty fellow
With ears that flap and flounder.
With bright yellow skin,
And knobbly chin,
And a nose like a quarter pounder.

POEMS FOR CHILDREN *(and silly people…)*

The Gumble Snoop is a bit of a rotter,
And prays upon slumbering tots.
Puts rumbles in tummies and pinches their toesies,
Wax in their ears and fills up their noseies.

Steals away dreams till the sleeping is done…
Yes, that Gumble Snoop – he's a bit of a one.

Your First Words

Your first word was *ga-ga*, or *goo*
With plenty of raspberries and giggles too.
With marmalade smiles and strawberry bubbles
Of goo-goo, gurgling and burgally boo.

Inch by inch, across the floor -
Tiny pinky caterpillar crawl -
Fluffy onesie and soft fuzzy dreams
With snuggly shmuggly cuddles for all.

My Imagination

You're entirely bonkers. But I'll tell you a secret:
All the best people are.

— Lewis Carroll

In my head there lies a book to astound
With pages well-thumbed and pictures abound:

Of mermaids and unicorns, steam trains and rockets,
With witches on broomsticks and giants with pockets
Of gold and diamonds mined from the sky,
Where the ghosts of summer float effortlessly by.

Rocking chairs, castles and gingerbread houses,
Magical pussycats chasing magical mouses.
Dinner parties, banquets and bendy balloons,
Gargoyles and dragons taking tea with baboons.

Candy floss forests and toffee apple pies,
Kaleidoscopic birds in kaleidoscopic skies.

Pelicans and piranhas on psychedelic pillows
With fluffy pink frocks on pirouetting hippos.

Castles and wizards on bicycles race
In a wizardry whirlwind with phenomenal pace.
In shards of images and chronicles compelling…
My noggin, is indeed, a very strange dwelling.

Frog

There is a frog in my garden
Who
        Hoppity-hops,
                Jumps and
                          Flops!
        Does belly splashes and flashes
From lily pad to
                          Lily pad
              To lily pad.
Then **SPLOSH!** Into the pond he dives.

He's damp and soggy - slippery little froggy.
Who ribbits and ribbits the whole night long.
He squats and burbles in google-eyed murmurs
In displays of frogginess and amphibious song.

I hear him at dawn as he sits on my lawn
Serenading a brand new day.
Breakfasting on bugs and pink slimy slugs
And butterflies that flutter his way.

Bubbles

My little girl loves bubbles,
    Or 'boobles!' as she exclaims

        'Flibble'
        'Flobble'
         'Wibble'

        'Wobble'

      Are all her favourite names.

    Drifting away - 'floaty flubbles'
Popping on roses –
Popping on noses –

Gleaming Squashy bubbles.

Little soapy faces
Vanish without traces,
Soaring higher and higher.
Beyond the shore –
Orbiting the Earth for evermore.

    Catch one in her hand
    And tries to climb inside -

POEMS FOR CHILDREN *(and silly people...)*

Where she could hide -
And waft away to another land.

Far, far away – beyond the moon
- In deepest darkest space
- A wobbly interplanetary place
Before the ship goes *BOOM!*

Little Lily Pinky

Little Lily Pinky let off a stinky
After a breakfast of boiled eggs and prunes.
- The dog got a bit sniffy
- And left in a jiffy.
And took refuge in his master's front room.

Little Lily Pinky had a re-thinky
After breakfasting on baked beans and veal.
- The wallpaper would curl
- And her brother would hurl
And the hamster drop dead in its wheel.

Beards

There was an Old Man with a beard,
Who said, "It is just as I feared!—

Edward Lear

Beards are so much fun,
With lots of things to find.
They tickle tummies and scratch at knees
And are great to hide behind.

A beard is a veritable treasure trove
With lots of trinkets to please,
From funny smells and sticky bits
To tiny crumbs of cheese.

I've found bits of old crumpets
And fragments of frozen peas,
Globules of gummy gravy
And lots of bouncy fleas.

A round of corned beef sarnies
And a smidgeon of Irish stew;
Some fragments of dried yoghurt
And some unrecognisable goo.

A beard provides a shelter
For loads of little beasties
Who come and go and ebb and flow
And bask in blobs and sneezes.

BARRY ROBINSON

I harbour lots of little furry things
And the occasional gnu,
Numerous twitters and tweeters
And herds of antelope too.

Beards are nice and fuzzy
And protect you from the sun,
Entangle lots and lots of tiny tots…
Yes… beards are so much fun!

Cucumbers

Cucumbers are gloriously silly,
Knobbly and long -
And always belong -
In my shopping trolley.

Cumbers are remarkably funny,
Lengthy and green –
And a little obscene -
And adored by ravenous bunnies.

Cucumbers are undeniably dreamy,
With tomatoes and dill -
They'll give you the chills -
With dressings to make them all creamy.

Snoring away in veggie slumber,
Lines and lines of queuing cumbers -
Stacked in indeterminable numbers -
Purposefully journeying unencumbered.

Little Tommy Tumpkins

"I'm so rumbly in my tumbly."

Winnie the Pooh

Little Tommy Tompkins had a rumble in his tumpkins
Which gurgled and murmured the whole day long.

He ate:

    Kippers and dippers, nutmeg and rice,
    Plum cake with syrup and sugar mice.

    Strawberry meringue with plenty of tang,
    Chicken with stuffing and blueberry muffins.
    Treacle tart with plenty of custard.
    Spicy noodles with oodles of mustard.

    Halibut and salad bits all crunchy and crisp.
    With green leaves and dressing with a lemony twist.
    Tea from the samovar, saveloys and thyme.
    Sweet meats in gravy and pilchards in brine.

    Puddings and biscuits with plenty of crumblings.
    Cabbages and cauliflowers and jars of onions.
    Olive-stuffed trout and freshly baked bream.
    Pastries and puddings, jelly and cream.

POEMS FOR CHILDREN *(and silly people...)*

Apple strudels and raspberry flan.
Freshly backed tarts with plenty of jam.
Dips and sauces with cheese and pickle.
Brussels and beetroot and beans that tickle.

Apples and oranges and freshly-picked lemons.
 Baguettes and croissant and buns with cinnamon.
Pancakes with drizzling and toad in the hole.
Crispy baked salmon and Jersey sole.

Buttered potatoes and runcible spoons.
Humbugs and jelly beans and punnets of prunes.
Pasties and poppadums and savoury pies.
Candy floss and sherbet all fizzy and dry.

Chutney and chilies with sultanas and fishes,
All pickled and fried in buttery dishes.
Sausages and fossages and fondant and foo.

One more bite...
And *POP!* Goes you.

He Gave Names to the Animals

And Adam gave names to all cattle, and to the fowl
of the air, and to every beast of the field;

Genesis 2:20

He gave names to all the animals
When he had nothing better to do,
From the humble flea to the bumble bee
And put the bounce in kangaroo.

'Elephant' ... hmmm, seemed irrelevant
And hippopotamus seemed obvious
(As his potomus was hip).

Zebra (or Zeeee – bra)
Were in their pyjamas, and llamas
Were like camels but calmer
(And not so spitty).

Wasps that sting and flappy things
He called geeses, and little furry bits called meeces.

Things that wriggle and squirm
Slippery swimmers and squiggly worms.

Crawly caterpillars and hairy gorillas.

POEMS FOR CHILDREN *(and silly people...)*

Racoons and baboons.
Dogs and frogs.
Turtles and purtles (or parrots perhaps).
Octopuses and stripy pusses.

From the roarers to the squeaky,
The scaly to the beaky.
All labelled in boxen,
Gnus, yaks and oxen,
Stomping and dancing with a fiddle-de-dee,
All adding to the bovine inventory.

They all sprang from the same clay
All in the span of a single day.
In 24 hours he'd named all the flowers,
And the swimmy things that live in the sea.
And finally he rested (on Sunday no doubt)
With freshly baked biscuits and tea.

Snuggly Shmuggly Boo

Snugly shmuggly boo
Lying next to you
Feet nice and toastie,
With ten little toesies
Snugly shumuggly boo.

Spiders are funny

Some the size of bananas,
Some the size of peas
Eight little hairy runners,
With forty-eight little knees.

They spin and spin
And hang on threads
   That descend
      Tumble
         Decline
           And fall.
Surfing the thermals of sequential snores.

Spiders are funny with face-hugging webs,
That stick to beards and freshly washed faces,
With strings of spidery straggly bits,
In the most inconvenient places.

Gathering gnats, beetles, moths and bees,
Ants, wasps, flies and fleas.
Harvesting all the bugs that pass by
All of them baked in a humungous fly pie.

Spiders are funny,
But cause such a fright-
When they jump out from nooks
And tickle faces at night.

Spiders are funny and cause such a kerfuffle.
They pitter and patter with a scampering scuffle.
Tittering and skittering with a trill little laugh,
Skating around the edges of the old tin bath.

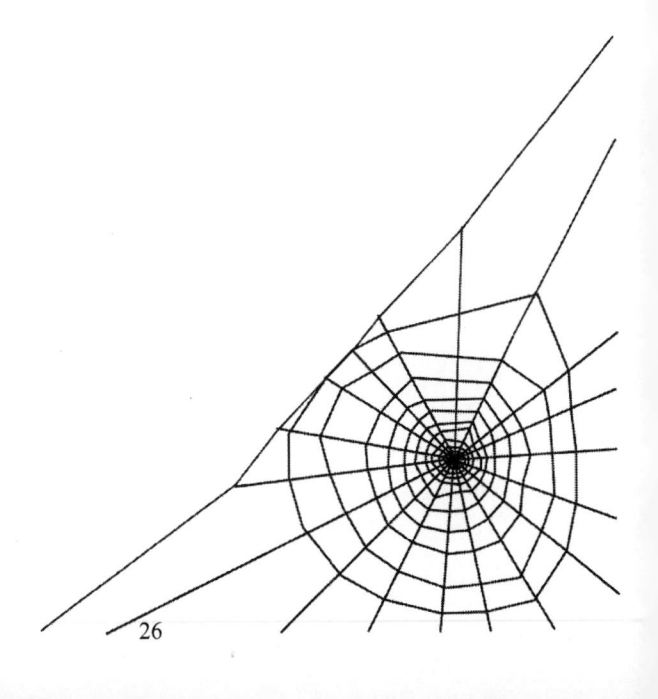

My Neighbour's dog

My neighbour's dog is a monster
Who gobbles up posties and small doggies.
He does whatever he wants to,
And lunches on itinerant moggies.

My neighbour's dog is a bruiser,
Who howls at the moon in the night.
He pees on the Vicar's begonias
And gives the bin men a helluva fright.

My neighbour's dog is a stinker,
Who enjoys small children on toast.
He gobbles up toddlers with relish
But prefers snotty boys the most.

My neighbour's dog died last night –
The cats let out a boisterous *'HOORAY!*
They partied well into the deep, dark night,
With champers and a shell-fish buffet.

The Knights of Foozalah
(A tale of Chivalry and Sausages)

The knights of Foozalah were noble and brave
And their pants were so stainless and pressed.
They burnished their armour and sharpened their swords
Awaiting their next knightly quest.
Their horses were saddled and the crowds they did throb
For a glimpse of Barnabas, Bartholomew and Bob.

They rode through the city, fearless and bold
As their steads cantered the well-trotted course.
They had begun their quest for the golden sausage
Until a log left poor Barnabas unhorsed.
Unseated and displaced he promptly bemoaned
The treacherous trail that left him dethroned.

Hills they did climb and streams traversed,
To the wood of the ghastly shadows;
Where the souls of the vanquished nightly cry
To unsettle the will in spine tingling bellows.
In the solemn darkness the dead did creep
As the Knights of Foozalah did soundly sleep.

POEMS FOR CHILDREN (*and silly people...*)

In the darkness of the forest a monster did wander.
In the darkness of the forest a monster did scoop
Unguarded jelly beans from the pockets of children
This fiend was the wangling trouser snoop.
Orange of eye and purple of bottom,
He would not rest until he'd got 'em.

But the knights of Foozalah were prepared.
The Knights of Foozalah lay in wait,
And pelted their enemy with pilchard sarnies
And left the poor fellow in a frightful state.
He thrashed and floundered until overrun,
Left crestfallen and fishy and categorically out done.

Our three brave knights gathered provisions –
Cinnamon buns from the baker, scotch eggs and pies –
And continued along their path to glory
To claim their much sought-after prize.
They rode, they gamboled amid playful banter
As their horses maintained a steady canter.

They searched every wood, every glade and valley.
They rode through the night and they rode by day
Until halted by a mire that bubbled and squelched
And puffed out vapours that would gurgle and spray.
The swamp was immeasurable – a noisome brew
Of boogers and belches and oceans of poo.

They thought and wondered how to traverse,
And all in unison on the muddy bank did kneel,
And prayed to the Goddess of crusaders
The hallowed way forward to reveal.
Then miraculously in one resounding fart
The malodourous ooze did begrudgingly part.

The Knights of Foozalah rode into the night
Their quest had reached its final round.
The rode into the mountain range
Where the golden sausage would be found.
There a cave of sighs, ominous and deep;
A fearful dragon - a fearful watch did keep.

The dragon was horrid and scaly.
The dragon was ferocious and strong.
He bellowed out flames and sulphur
And, by Jove, he didn't half pong!
Our heroes had the monster in their sights.
Our heroes were primed for the fight.

Brave Barnabus did step to the fore,
And from his saddle produce a violin.
With a mournful refrain and dulcet tones,
A beguiling music did Barnabus begin.
He played and played until his heart did soar
He played and played until he could play no more.

POEMS FOR CHILDREN *(and silly people…)*

The music spread across the valley -
Such mellifluous notes and tender refrains -
The dragon swayed in perfect unison,
With sweet vibrations and melodic strains.
Gentle cadences by gentle fingers wrung,
Like the songs of children sweetly sung.

The dragon shuddered, consumed with sadness
By past memories of vanquished foes.
He remembered faces of half-eaten children
Which populated his dreams and tweaked his nose.
The dragon stopped and said with a shiver:
"I miss me mum!" he bawled, all of a-quiver.

There was much a-weeping from the dragon
Such lamentations – as the beastie did bawl.
He was consumed by the desire to mend his ways
And waved the knights by, one and all.
The knights passed with a knightly wink
Their horses neighed and their armour chinked.

The golden glow lit up their noble faces.
A journey embarked upon at their king's behest.
The sort after sausage looming before them,
They worshipped the object of their quest.
Bartholomew held the sausage up high
As it punctured the darkness of the sky.

They rode through the kingdom to much tumult
As cheers poured forth from the admiring throng,
With banners aloft and flags flying high,
The three knights adored in celebratory song.
They waved and gestured to the delighted crowd
Replete with maidens with many gifts endowed.

The knights discussed their knightly valour,
And congratulated themselves on an outstanding job.
Their deeds were recorded in the knightly chronicles
Under 'Adventures of Barnabas, Bartholomew and Bob.'
Statues were erected, with bunting from trees
As our valiant heroes ate sausage sarnies for tea.

The Planets

Jupiter, or 'Poop-i-ter' (as my son calls it)
Because it's made up of smelly gas.
With several moons
Around it strewn
That never each other pass.

Neptune is a blue balloon –
Eighth in line to the sun.
With fourteen moons
And numerous monsoons
That beneath Triton are spun.

Mercury – the closest to the sun
Is hotter than Benidorm in June.
With no moons or rings
It habitually swings
Around like a little silver spoon.

Saturn is another gas giant
Where the weather is frightfully windy.
Composed of helium and hydrogen
Which we visit now and then
And float around like lunar debris.

Now Mars is the red planet,
With iron-rich craters and dust
Where terrible sand storms
Are regrettably the norm
But the view from the volcano's a must.

Uranus is a funny old planet
That often gets frightfully chilly.
Oberon, Titan, Mirander
All have a gander
But to stay would be awfully silly.

Venus is the goddess of love,
And reigns as the morning star.
It is dreadfully hot
And sizzles a lot
It's so bright it can be seen from afar.

Earth is where we all live,
With its oceans evenly spread.
I know it sounds drastic
But we're drowning in plastic.
So we'll all live on Jupiter instead.

Poooo-ey!

My Teacher's a Cannibal

I've eaten them raw in their holiday suits;
I've eaten them curried with rice...

Charles E Carryl

My teacher's a cannibal
Who nibbles on children all day:
She munches,
And brunches,
And crunches
All the little bones away.

Naughty boys are the best,
Especially with fresh bread and jam.
Little girls are nice (sugar and spice)
Wrapped in honey-roast ham.

Flesh sizzles and spits on a griddle.
The bones are boiled up for soup.
They suck and simmer,
Burble and shimmer,
Into one unwholesome bubbly gloop.

The older ones and a little bit chunky
And need to be tenderised and flayed;
Served with carrots and peas,
And a platter of cheese,
And a brittle tiny-tot sorbet.

Tiny little fingers – she dips in ginger
Accompanied by a pot of hot tea.
With biscuits and cakes she endlessly bakes
And voraciously gobbles with glee.

With a fine weathered wine
She passes the time
And *BURRRPS!* as she raises a glass.
She's smug and self-centred -
And always contented -
As she's sure her children will pass.

Book of Nonsense
(Dedicated to Mr Lear)

BARRY ROBINSON

Old Miss Hipkiss

(Inspired by an Edward Lear sketch)

Dear old Miss Hipkiss,
Had an enormous proboscis,
Which led the way to school.
It went over and over
Her best friend's shoulder
And dropped little emerald jewels.

It was decidedly iffy
When Mrs Hipkiss got sniffy
And sneezed with a resounding '*ahhhchooo!*'
Everyone bounded -
As the expulsion resounded -
With such a hullabaloo.

Such an incredible sniffer
Could eek out a whiffer
From as far away as China
One almighty snort,
Could easily contort,
The fault lines of North Carolina.

Her enormous appendage
Often upended
And caused a terrible rumpus.
Motorists were halted -
And her bugle insulted -
Despite being an excellent compass.

She married one day
To a prince from Bombay.
Her snooter protruded the vestibule.
Instead of confetti,
The guests tossed spaghetti,
Or anything deemed acceptable.

She died in the spring -
And much sadness did bring -
As her nose was famed in the land.
She was revered by the people,
And her snoot formed the steeple
Of a church built by royal command.

The Owl & the Pussy Cat

(The continuing adventures of)

The Owl and the pussy cat don't get on
And decided to call it a day.
They took some honey and plenty of money
To their lawyer who lives up the way.
The owl looked up to the stars above
And sang to the same guitar.
"O ghastly Pussy! O Pussy, you brute,
What a flea-bitten Pussy you are,
-You are,
-You are.
What a flea-bitten Pussy you are!"

Pussy sneered at Owl, "You despicable fowl!
How frightfully tuneless your song!
Too long we have tarried, not to be married
And I cannot bear to prolong."
For a year and a day, they sailed away
To the land where the Bong-Tree grows
For now it has withered and Piggy-Wig dithered

With two fingers pinching his nose,
His nose,
His nose.
With two fingers pinching his nose.

"Dear Pig, are you willing to buy for one shilling
This ring?" Said the Piggy, "I shan't."
So they cast it away, and were divorced the next day
By an aardvark who lived with his aunt.
They were finally allowed, and disavowed,
Their marriage in the midst of a dune.
With a glass of sherry and a resounding raspberry,
They parted by the light of the moon,
The moon,
The moon.
They parted by the light of the moon.

More Nonsense

There was a young doctor from Poole
Who lived upon bread and gruel.
She had butterflies in her tummy,
Whenever she spent money,
That funny young doctor from Poole.

The was a strange man from Reading,
Who had pigeon feathers for bedding.
He lived in a box,
That smelt of old socks,
That awfully strange man from Reading.

There was an old lady from Wigan,
Who discovered a brand new religion.
She worshiped the sun,
And homemade cream buns,
That funny old lady from Wigan.

There was an old lady from Dorset,
Who wore a chicken bone corset.
She puffed out a wish,
With a squeeze and she squish,
That strange old lady from Dorset.

There was young man from Chester
Whose beard would swarm and fester.
He called it a haven,
For a flea-bitten raven,
That shaggy young man from Chester.

There was an old man from Bourne,
Whose suit was all tattered and torn.
There were holes at the knees,
And a terrible breeze,
That plagued the old man from Bourne.

POEMS FOR CHILDREN (*and silly people...*)

There was an old lady from Eccles,
Whose knees were covered with freckles.
She entertained tots,
By joining the dots,
That strange old lady from Eccles.

There was a young man from Chorley,
Who always felt terribly poorly.
He smelt of blue cheese,
And tended to sneeze,
That ailing young man from Chorley.

There was a young lady from Crewe,
Whose breath smelt of pilchards and glue.
She entertained doodles,
Of aardvarks and poodles,
That awfully strange lady from Crewe.

There was a young man from Strood,
Whose trousers were terribly rude.
They made funny sounds,
As he walked around town,
That funny young man from Strood.

BARRY ROBINSON

There was a young lawyer from Brig,
Whose ears were incredibly big.
They'd flap and they'd blunder,
And lift him asunder,
That airborne you lawyer from Brigg.

There was an old spinster from Cheadle,
Whose knees were like two knitting needles.
They clattered and chimed,
And occasionally rhymed,
That noisy old spinster from Cheadle.

Nursery Rhymes
The Dead Sea Scrolls

# BARRY ROBINSON

Dr Foster

Doctor Foster went to Gloucester on the two thirty train.
The train was delayed so the good doctor stayed,
And never came home again.

Doctor Hester went to Leicester to buy himself some dill.
He had a curry but left in a hurry,
And neglected to settle his bill.

Doctor Thornball went to Cornwall to try some whelks and muscles;
When he got there the markets were bare,
As they'd all been shipped to Brussels.

Hey Diddle Diddle

Hey diddle diddle the cat's on the fiddle,
While the crickets chirped Clare de lune.
The silly dog grinned,
As the mice made a din,
And rocketed off to the Moon.

They played football with peas
And dreamt of the cheese,
While the cats cited Chairman Meow.
But the ship subsided as the rocket collided
With Farmer McTrumper's prize cow.

Hickery Dickery Dock

Hickery dickery dock,
The mouse has broken the clock.
The hand doesn't spin,
And the cuckoo stays in.
Hickery dickery dock.

Hickery dickery dock,
The mouse has run amok.
The clock doesn't chime
Or tell the time.
Hickery dickery dock

Hickery dickery dock,
He's on the chopping block.
With the farmer's wife,
And her big carving knife.
Hickory dickery dock

Hickery dickery dock,
The clock has finally stopped.
There are no furry feet,
To tap out the beats.
Hickory dickery dock.

Humpty Dumpty

Humpty Dumpty was a bit of a numpty
And decided to climb up a wall.
With no regard for his safety,
He felt a tad shaky
And cried out with a deafening yawl.

He floundered and tumbled and fell in a jumble,
And damaged the top of his noggin.
The emergency services were completely impervious,
And recommended a merciless flogging.

Incy Wincy Spider

Incy Wincy spider
Didn't know what to do.
He slid into the bath tub
but forgot to bring shampoo.
He couldn't find his loofah,
To scrub his underbelly.
So poor old Wincy went home again
Feeling rather smelly.

Jack & Jill

Jack and Jill went up the hill
To buy a pack of noodles;
The shop had none so Jack went home
And gave nothing to the poodles.

Up Jill got, and away did trot,
To get the poodles their tea.
She gave Jack a good thrashing,
And the poodles got lashings,
Of mash potatoes and peas.

Jack be Nimble

Jack was nimble and jack was quick,
But couldn't jump over the candlestick.
He fell mid-flight as the flame licked higher
And now he sings two octaves higher.

Jack was foolish and jack was silly,
Now his voice is falsetto and shrilly.
He legs are wobbly and his eyes are dimmer,
And he shuffles about with the aid of zimmer.

Little Bo Peep

Little Bo Peep has lost her sheep
Somewhere near Covent Garden.
They popped out for a curry,
Left a note: 'Not to worry'
And Bakerloo far behind them.

Little Bo Peep has found her sheep
In a cinema near Leicester Square.
She went for a peep,
But the prices were steep,
So they decided to go elsewhere.

Little Miss Muffet

Little Miss Muffet sat on a tuffet
Eating her bread and jam.
Along came a baboon,
With a large wooden spoon,
Prompting Miss Muffet to scram.

Little Miss Muffet sat on her tuffet,
Eating some custard creams.
Along came a flea
And sat on her knee
Causing Miss Muffet to scream.

Little Miss Muffet sat on a tuffet
Eating her rhubarb pies.
Along came a parrot
Who enjoyed a good claret,
Served with unboiled eggs and fries.

Mary, Mary

Mary, Mary quite contrary
How does your garden grow?
With lots of glue and kangaroo poo
And a weary old man with a hoe.

Sing a Song a Sixpence

Sing a song a sixpence
A pocket full of gherkins
Four and twenty dachshunds
All stuffed into firkins.
When the casks was opened
The hounds began to whine,
Upsetting all the serving maids
Who'd just sat down to dine.

The king was in the kitchen
Eating bread and dripping
The Queen was in the parlour
Practising her knitting
The maid was in the garden
Hanging out the clothes
When along came a gerbil
And nibbled at her toes.

The Grand Old Duke of York

The Grand old Duke of York.
He had a vindaloo.
He danced and pranced his way to a hedge,
To the clatter of his favourite tattoo.

His men had all decamped,
And made a ballyhoo
After eating all the poppadoms
And mango chutney too.

This Little Piggy

This little piggy went to Sainsbury's
And made canapés for tea.
And this little piggy had some camembert
And this little piggy had brie.
And this little piggy went *Oui, Oui, Oui*
To Normandy across the sea.

This little piggie had sausages
And this little piggie had brine.
This little piggy sour krout
And this little piggy had wine.
And this little piggie went *Ya Ya Ya*
To Dusseldorf via the Rhyne.

This little piggy had ravioli
This little piggie had spaghetti.
This little piggie had olives
And this little piggy had cappelletti.
This little piggie went *si si si*
All the way to Scandicci.

A Sweet Tooth

Barney Trundel had a bundle
Of cash to spend on sweeties:

Gobstoppers
And fruit poppers.

Lemonade pearls
And vanilla swirls.

Fizzy tips
And sugary bits.

Pear drops
And lollipops.

Sugar mice
And cosmic spice.

Liquorish and Space dust,
And packets of chewies fit to bust.

Caramel drums
And bubble gum.

Sherbet fountains
And insurmountable mountains
Of yumminess and gummy bears.

Jaffa cakes
And toffee bakes.

Chocolate dreams
And strawberry creams.

Humbugs and minty chews
And bags of slushy, sticky goo.

A whole quart rhubarb & custards
That grind away and erode his bicuspids.

All types sugary depravities…
And lots and lots and lots of cavities.

Pies are Great!

Pastry parcels for little tums.
Meat or veg and plenty of plums.
Served with custard, gravy and mash;
Rhubarb, cream or perhaps a dash
Of Worcester sauce for a little bite.
Crispy toppings, fluffy and light!

Pies are full of bacon and full of cheese.
Steak and kidney with broccoli and peas.
Chicken and mushroom and big chunky chips.
 Sweetcorn and pickles - an assortment of dips.

Fruit pie and fish pie
Deep-filled dish pie.

Humble pie and bumble-berry pie
Shepherd's Pie and strawberry pie

Lemon meringue pie
and Bedford clanger pie.

Pot pie and eel pie
Pork pie and veal pie.

Steak and ale pie
Cabbage and kale pie.

Meat pie
Cornish pie
Archimedes' pi –

Phew!
Pies are great!

Five Sisters

Amina flamina shamina boo,
Rode to school on a digeridoo.
With lots fuffle and hullabaloo,
Aamina flamina shamina boo.

Little Miss Maisy was a little bit hazy
With algebra, shmalgebra and pi.
She hated partitioning, and all the other things
Her teachers forced her to try.

Little Miss Abbie's
Hamster was flabby,
On a diet of cheese and choc dippers.
He keeled over one day
And slumped in the hay,
And now serves as excellent slippers.

Emily Sh-mem-illy shmoo,
Loved eating glutinous stew.
When she bunged up her teeth
Her dentist cried: "Good grief!"
And sent her to the back of the queue.

BARRY ROBINSON

Little Miss Lacy was incredibly pacey
Especially when she'd sausages for tea.
She'd sprint and she'd dash
For dollops of mash
And a spoonful of tinned mushy peas.

Christmas Acrostic

Crackers pulled with festive cheer.
Holly to mark the passing year.
Rolls of wrapping for all the toys.
Initialed stockings for girls and boys.
Snowmen and reindeer and Christmas kisses.
Tinsel and letters to Father Christmas.
Mistletoe and stuffing and drams of mulled wine.
Advent calendars and Auld Lang Syne.
Spices pies and yummy dishes…

Time with family and Christmas wishes.

Bottoms are Funny

Bottoms are funny
And occasionally smelly.
Wholesome family entertainment
Before we had telly.

They splutter and squeak
At the most inopportune places
Provoking disapproving grimaces
On disapproving faces.

A warm and comfy cushion -
On a bitter, frosty day.
That heats cold seats and trousers
In the most amusing way.

Goldilocks Got an ASBO

The three bears went for a wander
To let their porridge cool.
When along comes a girl called Goldilocks
Who thought she fancied a brew.

She climbed in through the bathroom window
And mischievously eyed up their crib.
She gobbled up all the porridge
And the pickles from the fridge.

She drank all the apple juice,
And felt a little bit squiffy -
Served up some pan-fried kippers -
Which made the house a bit whiffy.

She de-feathered the cushions
And broke up all the chairs,
She played on baby bear's x-box
And put banana skins on the stairs.

She turned on all the taps.
Squeezed toothpaste tubes in the middle.
Left a ring of grime in the bath
And the toothbrushes in a muddle.

She unmade all of the beds,
And unplumped all the pillows.

BARRY ROBINSON

Dropped crumbs between the sheets
And picked all the daffodilos.

Goldilocks stays at home these days,
Calling an end to her mischief and capers.
Never contravening her restraining order
And has her face in all of the papers.

I Wish I Were a Tree

I wish I were a tree
With bright shiny conkers,
Renewing every spring –
(Now there's the thing!)
Although it does sound a tad bonkers.

But my foliage would always be healthy.
My leaves would never fall out.
I'd have big sturdy branches
For squirrels with munchies
And furry things running about.

And my bough would never bend
As my branches swayed in the breeze
I'd provide sanctuary for kings*
And feathery things
I'd be the envy of all the other trees.

---

*Oak apple day is held on the 29th May. An English public holiday to commemorate the restoration of the English monarchy in May 1660. Legend has it that Charles II hid in an Oak tree near Boscobel House to escape detection by the Roundhead army.

Making Lists

I like making lists. It's a bit of an obsession.
All my good deeds and all my transgressions:

Everything that needs to be done
On my list - one by one.

Everything I want to eat,
All my emails – all my tweets.

Everybody I need to call,
In one indecipherable scrawl.

Cities I will visit one day,
Trips to places far away.

All the dreams that flit through my head,
And all the boxes under my bed.

Holidays I wish to take -
And all the lists I need to make.

Making lists helps me sleep -
Once I've tired of counting sheep.

Woolly jumpers – one by one
Bleat and gambol when the day is done.

POEMS FOR CHILDREN *(and silly people…)*

But when I'm tucked up tight in bed -
The interminable day's woes are shed…

I prefer to draft my lists instead.

The Marillos

The Marillos weave elaborate tapestries
Of ocean clouds and sunset towns.
Asylum satellite – round and round
An intricate interplay of light and sound.

The Marillos are unusual beasties,
With Moog and Wurlitzer complete.
Visitations from Planet Marzipan
Strains of lavender and Dreamy Street.

*The Marillos are itinerant players, who gather in Leicester biannually, bringing with them a collection of oddities and ne'er-do-wells.

Our Little Snorer

My little boy snores and snores
And trumpets and roars.
Sawing up logs all through the night.

He rasps -
And gasps -
And breezes -
And wheezes.
He shuffles -
And snuffles.

The hullabaloo is preposterous -
Like a bad tempered rhinoceros -
That echoes from room to room.

The doors they do slam
And the curtains they billow.
His nostrils they flare
And suck up the pillows.

He must not have dairy
We must be vigilant and wary

Of anything pulsy or bilious.
Lentils and sprouts must all be left out
Or we plagued with all snorts and silliness.

So he's every so mindful of foods to refuse,
And has a list of grub he avoids.
But Just one crumb of cheese or a spoonful of peas,
And he's like a silver back gorilla on steroids.

The Greedy Puss

Platypus was a fatty puss who gobbled up all the fish.
He lapped up the cream and slices of bream,
But haddock was his favourite dish.

He purred and mumbled in soft pulsating rumbles
After a supper of sardines and crab.
He'd snore and shout and thrash about
Whilst dreaming of turbot and dab.

Platypus was a fatty puss who loved oysters and eel.
He was unpleasantly selfish when it came to shellfish
And apoplectic if you eye up his meal.

Princess Frog Snogger

Princess Frog Snogger was a bit of a slogger,
Who confessed to preferring toads:
*"They may be warty and little bit haughty
But they certainly don't get up my nose.*

Frogs are slimy and ever so grimy!" She whined.
*"They posture and preen, and their breath is obscene
Whenever they've recently dined.*

"They're ever so fickle and cause such a pickle!"
She exclaimed:
*"As they leap and bound with a croak.
They jump and they splash and are gone in a flash –*

Toads are definitely my type of bloke!"

Rhapsody in Pink

Fie-Fie Foo-Foo little girl,
Lost in bubbles, cuddles and curls.
She smiles and dances all summer long
With laughter and sweeties and sugar-tongs.

Fie-Fie Foo-Foo little girl,
All candy floss, giggles and raspberry swirls.
Gazing at clouds and moon mice at play
And giggling at ladybirds that barrel away.

Fie-Fie Foo-Foo little girl,
Journeys at night to magical worlds;
With dragons, fairies, fabled Queens,
Princesses, butter-cups and jelly beans.

Fie-Fie Foo-Foo little girl,
Tucked up snug in moonlit twirls.
Dreams of gooey things all chocolate and cream,
Skips through palaces that sparkle and gleam.

Sausages

Great big fat ones,
Popping in the pan ones.

Spicy ones
In buttered buns,
With oodles of sauce
And onions of course.

Cumberland sausages
Have many advantages,
But great big bangers are best.
With bread and butter -
Sets my heart a-flutter -
With sizzling sausagness blessed.

Great big pork ones,
Speared on my fork ones.
Grilled and smoked,
Fried and poked.
Served with peas and
Gravy soaked.

Enormous belt busters,
Smothered in mustard;
All from my secret sausage stash.
Lots of crispy crunchiness,
And savoury sausage munchiness,
Accompanied by gravy and mash.

Simile Song

As sober as a judge.
As drunk as a lord.
As free as a bird.
As stiff as a board.

As cool as a cucumber.
As busy as a bee.
As clean as a whistle.
As slippery as an eel.

As gentle as a lamb.
As mad as a hornet.
As fit as a fiddle.
As pretty as a bonnet.

As white as snow.
As warm as toast.
As black as coal.
As clear as a ghost.

As jolly as a sand-boy.
As warm as clover.
As sweet as a nut…
Our poem is over.

Teddington

Teddington sits at the end of the bed,
Listening to the snores and roars
Of midnight ambles to far off lands.

Big ears, squishy and fuddled,
And early morning cuddles.
And smiles from marmite faces
Sticky with traces
Of breakfast and kisses –
Bruises - near misses
Of playground bumps and grazes.
Worn out knees and threadbare blazers.

Teddington sits at the end of the bed.
Listening to soft exhalations
and whispered declarations
Of love, sweet dreams
And goodnight wishes.

Smile Train

*Smile train visits far-flung places
Delivering beamers to tiny bright faces.

Barrelling along at an alarming rate.
Clickety-clack – no time to wait!

Moonbeams and rainbows to guide its way
To those in need of a smile today.

Trundling from Delhi to Mangalore,
Bringing smiles and so much more.

*Smile Train is a charity that provides essential treatment for children in developing countries enabling them to access cleft pallet surgery. They bring smiles to lots of bright little faces. Check out their website: smiletrain.org

Terrence Rex

Terrence lives at the back of my garden.
He stomps, chomps, and thunders about
Eating pussycats and brussel sprouts.

He hollers in the morning
wakes all the neighbours,
Trampling the shrubs
And watering the azaleas.

Dinosaur poo
Sticks like glue
To sploshes
And galoshes
To roses
And toeses.

With bellowing roars -
And poo beleaguered claws -
He announces himself with distinction.
We cower in holes -
Like timid little voles
And pray for a meteoric extinction.

Snowflakes

Snowflakes flutter – dissolve
Like memories -renewing
In soft flurries
Of crisp whiteness.

Hot steaming mugs
And fingerless gloves –
Breathing in wispy clouds
Of exhalations - unfurling
On the glacial air.

Snowflakes shimmer
Like Christmas lights
And children's laughter
On frosty December
Mornings…

Summer Days

Summer days are full of ways
Of languishing in early morning rays
Of summer sun.

With buzzy bees and leafy trees
Full of fruit and summer flowers
For hours spent in their shade,
With glasses of lemonade,
And iced tea, naturally.

Freshly mown lawns and dawns
Of crisp golden sunrise.
With dreams
Of Cornish cream,
On summer days where children play.

Before autumn rain comes to stay,
In shivering upon shivering ranks of grey.

Fingers McFilcher

Fingers McFilcher is a stealer of dreams,
And lingers beneath your bed.
He creeps and he peeps when you're asleep
and rummages around in your head.

He carries around a brown paper bag -
Unicorns, gingerbread and bows,
Which his bony fingers pinch and pull
With resounding POP! from your nose.

He holds them up for inspection,
Then adds to his collection
Of dreams about:

Silver rings and fluffy things,
Candyfloss and fairies.

White sandy beaches and syrupy peaches,
Brownies and stinky mud pies.

Fabulous journeys with twist and turnies;
Trumpeting pachyderms, pocket-rifling monkeys

Cowboys and Indians and Wild West shenanigans,
Wagon wheels and blueberry flans.

BARRY ROBINSON

Big yawny hippos and pink scrunchy pillows,
Fields of daisy pies and armadillos.

Sherbet fountains and snow-covered mountains
Freshly glazed plums and lots of toy drums.

Cops and robbers and jammy dodgers,
Big bumper cars and chocolate bars.

He limps with an old wooden cane -
And is clearly insane -
As he cackles his way round the house.
-If you wake he'll shout "boo!"
-And maybe take you!

So be as quiet as a snoozy little mouse.

Nicola Pickle-a

Nicola Pickle-a pilchards and pie
Stole some scones as the Queen rode by.
Some with butter and some with spread
Some with treacle and some with bread.

Nicola Pickle-a pudding and jam,
Sent some pizza by telegram.
She boxed it up and sent it away,
For her friend to eat the very next day.

Nicola Pickle-a porridge and kippers
Went to school in her mother's slippers.
She filled them with lavender, haddock and custard,
And smeared her toes with marmalade and mustard.

Widgity-Fidgity

Widgity-Fidgity, *fiddle-de-dee*.
Fiddled and fiddled whilst drinking her tea.
She pushed all the buttons and pulled at the bows
Unravelled the cotton and tweaked all her toes.
And when she was finished it started to rain,
And Widgity-Fidgity started again.

Widgity- Fidgity *fiddle-de-dum*.
Fiddle and fiddled while filling her tum.
She squished all the berries and scrunched all the bread;
Slurped all the ice-cream then stood on her head.
And when she was finished it started to rain
And Widgity-Fidgity started again...

The Mouse Thief

The wind was a torrent of darkness among the leafy trees,
Along crept the naughty mouse looking for some cheese.
The road was a ribbon of moonlight leading to the door,
And the hungry mouse came knocking –
    Knocking – knocking.
The hungry mouse came knocking, up at the old Inn door.

He'd a rumble in his tummy, a cravat up to his chin.
His boots were made of leather but wearing awfully thin.
He'd walked for miles over fields and styles for a sip of tea.
When he saw the light a-twinkling
    A-twinking – a-twinkling.
The inn light was a-twinkling, shining for all to see.

He desired camembert he even fancied brie.
He craved smelly fromage - he was a French mouse you see.
A window was left open and the shutters they did clatter,
    Clatter – clatter.
The shutters they did clatter, beneath the old ash tree.

He climbed through the window and feasted on the cheese,
He ate and ate and filled his belly with all his eyes could see.
He gorged himself and filled his tum and swiftly fell asleep
    Asleep – asleep.
He fell asleep as Black Paws (the inn cat) did creep.

When the moon is full and still, shining on travelers bright,
A ghostly squeak is heard in the stillness of the night.
A phantom mouse is whiskering, creeping upon a breeze
    Creeping – creeping.
The phantom mouse comes creeping, looking for the cheese.

The Sea

A man that is born falls into a dream, like a man who falls into the sea...

Joseph Conrad

Big, blue wobbly thing beneath the horizon
Where the fishes live.
Crashing and smashing,
Foaming and combing
The coastline - for little spots of rocks,

Left there – bereft and bare
Stripped from the greater part of itself –
Deposited upon the shelf of the morning tide.

The air thick with sprays of salt
That tingle on the tongue.

The distant hum of carousels and wurlitzers
The waft of chips unwrapped -
Kiss-me-quick hats with lipstick smudged
Whipped ice cream and hand-made fudge.

Halls of mirrors – shiver and shape.
Helter Skelters swirl and whirl –
Ever decreasing and ceasing with a bump.

BARRY ROBINSON

Gannets dance with the evening tide,
Sun sets against the illuminations – lighting
The great cathedrals of a fun-filled day.

A Train Journey

Caught the train at Tottenham -
To Barnsley via Windy Bottom.

Huntingdon to Paddington -
Then back and forth to Piddleton,
After lots of lemon tea.

Blackpool and Grimsby -
Clacking through Whittlesea.
Lincolnshire for sausages -
Yorkshire for puddings -
Melton Mowbray for pies -
Biscuits from Reading.

Stubbington and Dibbleson -
A short break in Darlington -
Bridlington and Poole -
Stotties from Newcastle -
And Curd Tarts from Goole.

Stopping off in Congleton -
Cream teas in Callington -
Sticky buns in Bungay -
Poodles in Bootle -
Bunting in Buntingford -
Cockles from Pocklington -
And B&B in Bridlington.

BARRY ROBINSON

Skegness and Ware -
Spalding and Boston -
And back down to Swindon -
And Western super Mare.

First class to Dewsbury -
Then elevenses in Shrewsbury -
Forty winks in Biggleton -
Wiggles in Wigglegton.

Waking up in Manchuria…
Gosh, what an adventure!

Vegetables

"I hate veggies!"
He huffed and puffed stubbornly.
"Carrots are yucky and cabbage is blurrrrr!
And don't get me started on broccoli!"

"No more peas with macaroni cheese
And spinach tastes just like snot!
I'm not eating cauliflower! I'm not eating swede!
You can take away the whole blooming lot!"

"I'm not eating aubergines
And beans make me toot.
And tomatoes are vegetables
Pretending to be fruit!"

"But sweet corn with butter
Is scrumptious and yummy!
Slips down like a treat and is ever so sweet,
And burbles away in my tummy!

Words

Words, words, words...

William Shakespeare

Words on balloons – banners and spoons;
Initials on forks and knives.
Cards for mummy and daddy and Aunty Sue
Words for fractured lives.

Words on walls say it all,
Two letters – three letters, four.
Messages on scrolls and toilet rolls,
Billet-doux tucked away in drawers,
Ribboned and hushed.

Poems dripping syllables,
Syrupy sweet,
With similes and silly bees
Buzzing onomatopoeically.

Dusty tomes in welcoming homes
Full of kisses and cheerios.
Princesses and pirates and maidens that call
For moustachioed heroes to rescue them all.

Words explosive and plosive
Pour from cards for broken hearts:

POEMS FOR CHILDREN *(and silly people…)*

- Invitations
- Salutations
- Commiserations

First words to last words
All pregnant with meaning.

Sounding resounding
Spaces to be in.

Words spoken and words unuttered
Hearts unpacked and attics decluttered.
Words of love and words of longing,
Our lives in words,
Our lives belonging.

To words expressed on pages
And words expressed verbally.
And when all is said and done,
We belong to words…
And words interminably.

I Love Pickles

I love pickles!
Big, green and ever so knobbly;
Onions and cucumbers and florets of broccoli,
With plenty of crunch – plenty of bite;
Contained in containers all scrumptious and tight.

I love pickles!
Jars and jars of vinegary yumminess
That burble and gurgle away in your tumminess.
Great in sarnies with slices of spam.
All served with tomatoes, jalapenos and jam.

I love pickles!
Especially the trumpy variety –
Served with cinnamon and spiced lemon tea,
Gherkins and beans and soft creamy cheese,
For heartburn and rumbles and that warm pickley
breeze.

My Toilet is Haunted

My toilet is definitely haunted!
By the ghost of a pirate buccaneer.
- With a resounding *"Ah- harrrrrr!"*
 - This annoying Jack Tar
Flushes whenever I'm near.

My Toilet is certainly haunted!
By a pirate that sailed the Bahamas.
- He leaves the towels in a heap.
 - And furtively creeps
And tugs at my stripy pyjamas.

My toilet is undoubtedly haunted!
By a Pirate named Captain Jack Bones.
- He looks for the treasures
 - In all kinds of crevices
Left by old Davy Jones.

My toilet is unquestionably haunted!
By a pirate that once walked the plank.
- *"Pieces of eight!"*
- His parrot did prate,
As into the Pacific he sank.

So now my toilet is haunted!
By a pirate with a big bushy whiskers,

BARRY ROBINSON

- My loofa he brandishes
- And curls all my sandwiches,
As *"Avast – scurvy dog"* he whispers.

"Ah- harrrrrr!"

Elephants

Elephants are great big trumpety things
Gorging themselves on sticky buns.
Piles and piles of pachyderm poo.
 Consuming bananas by the ton.

Elephants just love to shower
Aided by a gargantuan sponge.
A quart of shampoo and shower gel too
To shift that elephantine grunge.

Elephants all love to trumpet
And listen to free-form jazz
-   They tango all night
-   (Avoiding the mice!)
To that baggy-bottomed razzmatazz.

Cloud Gazing

Clouds are great big fluffy things
That live high up in the sky
Resembling faces and traces of places
That wander nonchalantly by:

Great antlered mooses
And flappy white gooses.

Big springy fleas
Silly bumbling bees.

Mermaids gamboling in oceans deep
And fields and fields of bleating sheep.

Skipping ropes, igloos and rhubarb pies
Totem poles, bicycles and butterflies.

Plumes and plumes of fluffy duck down
And endless processions of tumbling clowns.

POEMS FOR CHILDREN *(and silly people...)*

Puffins and penguins and squawky cockatoos
Llamas in pyjamas and bouncy kangaroos.

Elephants in tutus flying strawberry kites
Fire breathing dragons and ammonites.

Aubergines, porcupines cabbages and kings.
A firmament of swirls and magical things.

The End

The end of the day
We drift away
On words and phrases
To fabulous places...

If you, or your little ones, have enjoyed these poems please take a moment to leave feedback on amazon. It all helps sales.

A donation to Smile Train will be made for every copy sold.

Printed in Great Britain
by Amazon